The Railway Children – The mysterie

By Year 5

CW00839589

Dear reader,

This story continues from the last adventures of The Railway Children, where Father was sentenced to five years in jail. Thankfully, thanks to the kind Old Gentleman's help, Father is now back with the family.

Throughout this story, there will be many adventures and lots of twists and twirls, so read on to find out what happens next!

Yours sincerely,

Year 5

Harlaxton C of E Primary School

The railway children have been busy as always with their adventures. They live in a small but cosy house near the railway. Their house is two stories high and they live with their Mother and Father. It also has 2 beautiful bedrooms- one for the children and one for their parents.

On a hot, late summer afternoon, Bobbie, Phyllis and Peter decided to go on a walk in the forest. It was an enormous, dark forest and deep within was a track with wildflowers on either side and old debris, which looked like it could be from an old, steam train. As they started to walk along the rough, stoney path, Phyllis could hear a peculiar noise. "Can you hear that?" Phyllis whispered. "It sounds like rustling coming from those bushes." Phyllis wanted to turn back but the others wanted to explore.

Half an hour later, they decided to turn back as the weather was starting to turn. Grey clouds filled the sky. Rain was approaching. After a short while, they found a dog, but it had no name or owner- it was lost. He was very fluffy, chestnut brown dog that was as brown as a tree trunk, but they start having an argument about taking a stray dog home. Peter named it Timmy.

Like a bullet speeding through the air, Timmy charged through the forest and the children struggled to keep up. Excited to have found a new friend, the children take Timmy back home to their mother and father.

Chapter 2

By Oscar, Logan and Scarlett

As Peter, Bobby and Phyllis were walking home from the forest, they stumbled across an old track. The rusty track was damaged and overgrown with slippery, green moss and brambles sharp as knifes. Cautiously, they approached the track and found a rundown, spooky train. Peter, who was walking in front of Phyllis and Bobby, climbed into the train first. As he slowly opened the damaged door, CREEAAK! The children covered their ears.

They decided to investigate the eery carriages and go deeper into the darkness. Soon after, Peter started hearing faint crying noises. Startled, he found a baby boy wrapped in a ragged, blue blanket.

"Look!", cried Peter to his sisters, "There's a baby!".

"We must find his mother", Phyllis said nervously. Bobby picked up the baby and the four of them carried on through the carriages hoping to not find any further casualties. Suddenly, they discovered a woman lying on the floor.

"Do you think this lady could be his mother?", Peter asked.

The three children ran up to the lady. Filled with shock, they try to wake her, but she does not wake up. Peter, who was holding the young, crying baby looked at the mother. He noticed she was holding a letter. He anxiously looked up at Phyllis.

"A letter! I've found a letter!" shouted Peter.

As they head home, they enquire within the village for further information to see if anyone has noticed the track before. After their confidence kicked back in, they took the letter back to their mother, and she discovered that it was written in Russian. It wasn't long before the mother put two and two together and found out that it was the Russian man's family on the train.

Phyllis eventually asked Mother if she could find the Russian man. "You most certainly cannot", said the mother in an unusually shrill voice. Sadly, they didn't know where the Russian man went. After a few days of planning, the children decided to sneak out at the dead of night to find the Russian man to alert him about his wife and child.

The children made their way to the station hoping to talk to the old man. On their way, they went through multiple dark sodden tunnels with yawning mouths, and past a frog infested lake. For the most part, there was an eerie silence but as they approached the station, they could hear a noise. It was the stern voice of the old gentleman. Hoping to find answers, the children follow the voice to find him.

Chapter 4

By Ines, Jocelyn and Isaac

The children strolled through the sunlit street, leaves blowing, and a chill breeze pinching their skin making their way to the railway. They made it and questioned the old gentleman, eager to set off on their journey. Filled with excitement to start the search, they asked him where the Russian man went but he said that he didn't know much. He told them that he was heading to London but, he was not sure where he would be now. So, they thanked the man and headed away from the station, making their way back to the abandoned track. Where could he be?

They headed back to the train to update Bobby but, they took a wrong turn and got lost. In the corner of Peters eye he saw a man. He asked the man if he'd seen an abandoned train.

The man said, "I fixed a train not far from here." Suddenly, they heard a TOOT TOOT- a train was heading towards them. They ran towards the sound of the train, and they saw that the train had started moving. They ran after the train screaming and shouting but, Phyllis fell over and hurt her leg. Peter kept running and shouting and eventually, the train slowed down to a halt. Peter ran back towards Phyllis to help her up. Peter asked "Phyllis are you alright?"

"Yeah but it hurts" said Phyllis wincing as Peter examined the cut.

Peter and Phyllis heard two people talking, so they both looked up. Peter helped Phyllis up and helped her walk towards the train. As they got closer, they heard Bobby speaking to someone. They went inside the train and saw Bobby. "Oh Phyllis what have you done to you leg?" asked Bobby.

"Oh, I fell over." said Phyllis looking down at her muddy, bright red legs.

Chapter 5

By Victoria, Lily, George and Ethan

The children are amazed to see the mother, "Why are you awake?" said Bobby quietly.
'What d'ya mean?" she asked, face was filled with confusion.
'We thought you were dead as you were not waking up." exclaimed Phyllis quietly.
The children looked at each other, uncertainty filled their faces. Maybe the Russian man they had seen previously at the train station was a relation to this beautiful woman.
'I was searching for my husband because he left us so suddenly. I thought maybe he would be on his way to London to find work, as we did not want to end up in a workhouse. I was making my way there when suddenly... the train crashed!" The children decided they would help the lady to find her husband, they didn't want the baby to be away from its father.

Bobby turned to her siblings, "We need to help!"
The children set off on their journey. The ear-piercing whistles of the train could be heard as it slowly crept out of the station.

Chapter 6

By Caiden and Amy

After a long journey, they arrive into the grand station in London. The three siblings noticed how polluted the sky was compared to the countryside. The young, tired children found Victorian London muggy and full of cold mist. The smell of fumes from factories immediately jumped up their noses.

The three siblings were searching the streets of London when they bumped into a police man. His teeth were chattering as fast as lightening. They immediately felt intimidated. Something was wrong. Full of fear, the children were abruptly thrown into the back of a horse and carriage and taken to a dingy workhouse.

The children enter the conventional workhouse. They were scared and terrified. There was numerous torture chambers with frail and unclean workers, who were covered in blisters. Their hands were bleeding. The children hated the workhouse. They have never seen anything so ghastly and inhumane in their lives before.

Upon their arrival, the guardian informs them they will never see sunlight again and will be split up into boys and girls. "Hahaha! You will never escape this place!" laughed the strict guard with a mischievous grin plastered across his face. In the blink of an eye, Peter was taken to the boy's dormitory where the children were made to sleep four in a bed. Phyllis and Bobby were rushed to the girl's dorm and given strict instructions of the schedule for the rest of the day. Wishing they had taken a different route and escaped the guard, they get themselves prepared for a rough night. They take a quick look around then realise they can't escape because there is guards everywhere.

Peter meets a boy, in the boy's wing, called Oliver who had dark brown hair and deep green eyes. He tells Peter his very detailed escape plan. Little did they know, a guard was going to help them a little while later. "Come with me!" the guard whispered. Peter and Oliver follow him. "I will help you escape this prison!"

"Oh, thank you, thank you!" Peter and Oliver said together. The guard hands over a key. Peter looked at the key, puzzled. "What's the key for?" He asked.

"It is the key for the kitchen. In there is a window that is unlocked. That is your best exit out of here and you will not be seen." The man exclaimed. Peter recognises the man but cannot think why.

Panicking and full of fear, Peter and Oliver set off to find the kitchen. Peter, who was tip toeing in front of Oliver, heard a loud barking. A guard dog was around the corner. They snook across after almost getting caught and found the cafeteria. The two boys made sure they were as quiet as a mouse. The sound of the barking was getting louder. In a panic, Peter turned to Oliver, "Quick! Let's go!" They scuttled round the corner and ran into a guard. They scrambled back and managed to turn and run the other way. The boys hear a voice bellowing behind them. "Come back here right away!"

Meanwhile, Bobbie and Phyllis have been preparing food for the following day, which was made in an ancient, crooked kitchen where you could hear leaking pipes in the dingy workhouse, wondering how Peter is being treated. "Do you think Peter has made friends?" enquired Phyllis.

Bobbie replied, "Of course Peter has made a friend, he is very talkative."

"Bobbie why are we here... I want to go home," Bobbie did not respond as she did not know the answer and did not want to upset Phyllis further. She was supposed to be the big sister who took care of everyone.

Bobbie and Phyllis slowly made their way back from the kitchen towards their dormitory. They could not understand why their uniform was so uncomfortable; Bobbie knits with her mother back in Yorkshire and is used to soft, comfortable clothing. She could tell that the dirty, ragged dress was a depth of dark coarse material, which was itchy and frilly.

In the distance, the girls spot Peter talking to the guard. They try to listen.

The boys continue to talk to the Russian man and know that they could trust him and ask him if he can help them escape.

"How did you get here from being on the train looking for your wife?" Peter asked in wonder.

The Russian man replied, "I came to London to find my wife and baby boy. He turned two yesterday. Two guards grabbed me and pushed me into this miserable, crowded workhouse. I pleaded to become a guard instead of working and to my surprise, they said yes! So here I am". Suddenly, they were interrupted by a bang as loud as a bomb and Peter shouted, "What was that!"

The guard explained that it was a sound they often heard from the men working outside. Peter and Oliver continued to talk to the Russian man and realised that he wasn't like the rest of the guards. He explained that he tries to help people escape and that he would join the children in escaping.

From the distant corner, Phyllis whispers anxiously "Bobby did you see that! They look like they are making a plan to escape."

As Peter and Oliver implement their plan with the guard, who was the Russian man, Bobbie and Phyllis were back to work. They were trying to search for an easy escape in the workhouse for them all. Firstly, Peter and Oliver had to tell the girls their plan that they had made with the guard the previous night. The plan was to creep out of their dormitories and meet Bobbie and Phyllis at the dinner hall. All four children had to crawl down the dark, dingy corridor to their meeting point to discuss their escape plan. CREAAAAK. The door opened slowly. Suddenly, a mysterious figure walks into the dinner hall where the children are. It was the Master of the workhouse!!

"You naughty children! How dare you sneak out of your dormitory at night! You will be punished. The cane for you all".

With that, more guards turned up.

Bobbie and Phyllis distract the guards. They run into the back pantry and the guards follow them in. BANG! CLATTER! Pots and pans were being thrown in a panic to hit the guards. Peter and Oliver try to escape and run past the master as quick as lightening. The guards start chasing them down the hallway and leave Phyllis and Bobbie behind. The boys run as fast as their legs could carry them and they made it out the old workhouse through the front door. They run round the back of the building and find a small window to the room that Bobbie and Phyllis are hiding in. SMASH! Peter breaks the glass and climbs in to help the young girls out.

The Russian man, who was disguised as a guard, saw the young, distressed children and ran to them to help.

"Quick! Let's get out of here!" the Russian man waves his hand to get the children's attention. They turn and run as fast as they could towards the Russian man, and they all escape together. Eventually, they reach the rusty, old track to find his beloved wife and baby. When they got there, they discovered that the mother and baby had disappeared. "Where have they gone?" Phyllis said panicked.

"I think I have found them", Peter shouted from across the way. He saw them hiding under a tree. The woman looked up at the sound of their voices and saw her husband. She rushed over and hugged him so tight she thought she would never let go. They were so happy to see each other again! They all walked back towards the train station where they would travel back to Yorkshire. All they could hear was the rustle of the leaves on the ground.

Chapter 10

By Lauren and Joshua

The train slows to a squeaky halt in Yorkshire train station. The children are happy to be home. In the distance, they see the Russian family walking down the platform. The Russian man waved the children over and thanked the children for taking care of their adorable baby. He insisted on joining the children on their journey home so that he could explain to their parents what wonderful, heroic children they are.

The children arrived back home and were hugged by the warmth of the house, eating a delicious dinner and chit chatting away next to the bright orange, burning fire. The evening was soon over, and the Russian family thanked them for their company. As they walk out the door the children's mother said, "We love having you around you can come over anytime you like to have dinner again. It was lovely having you. Take care of yourself."

As the children got ready for bed, Bobby said to Peter and Phyllis "That was an adventures day!"

"Yes, it certainly was", said peter and Phyllis exhaustedly.

"Good night, sweet dreams", said Bobby.

"Good night", Peter and Phyllis replied together. They all fell fast asleep.

Printed in Great Britain
by Amazon

36236589R00015